OLD STOCK

ALADDIN

AND OTHER TALES FROM THE

ARABIAN NIGHTS

A DORLING KINDERSLEY BOOK

A RETELLING FOR YOUNG READERS BASED ON EARLY VERSIONS OF THE *ARABIAN NIGHTS*

Art Editor Sarah Stanley
Senior Editor Marie Greenwood
Design Assistant Tanya Tween
Research Fergus Day
Production Katy Holmes
Managing Art Editor Jacquie Gulliver
Picture Research Louise Thomas
DTP Designer Kim Browne
Consultant Dr Parween N. Arif,
Department of Arabic and Middle Eastern Studies, University of Leeds

First published in Great Britain in 1998 by
Dorling Kindersley Limited, 9 Henrietta Street, London WC2E 8PS

Visit us on the World Wide Web at http://www.dk.com

Text copyright © 1998 Rosalind Kerven

Illustrations and compilation copyright © 1998 Dorling Kindersley Limited

A CIP catalogue record for this book is available from the British Library.

ISBN 0-7513-7087-8

Colour reproduction by Bright Arts in Hong Kong
Printed by Graphicom in Italy

EYEWITNESS CLASSICS

ALADDIN

AND OTHER TALES FROM THE ARABIAN NIGHTS

Retold by
ROSALIND KERVEN

DORLING KINDERSLEY

LONDON • NEW YORK • STUTTGART • MOSCOW

Illustrated by
NILESH MISTRY

CONTENTS

Shahrazad   Shahryar

Dunyazad

Aladdin   The magician

Farizad

Ali Baba

Marjana

The fisherman

Introduction

The stories of the *Arabian Nights* began their life, many centuries ago, as oral folktales. They have survived countless retellings in many different times and places. They endure because they have a special, timeless quality – the power to strike a chord, to stir the imagination, and to hold an audience spellbound.

These tales were originally told, not to children, but to adults. The oldest written versions belonged to a much slower age – many of them were long, full of detailed description and philosophical reflections.

Today the stories are an essential part of children's culture. In simplified forms they have inspired films, cartoons, and pantomimes.

The retellings in this book, adapted from early versions, reflect the rich diversity found in the *Arabian Nights*. They include *Aladdin* – the best known and best loved of all the tales – the lyrical *Garden of Enchantments*, and the humorous and thrilling *Ali Baba*. The special quality of this Eyewitness Classic is to bring to life the medieval Islamic world of the tales. Photographs and paintings help us to understand their cultural context, while the enchanting illustrations – influenced by Persian art – capture their marvellous, complex magic. For as Shahrazad herself shows in the first tale, powerful stories can change people; they can also live forever.

Shahrazad telling stories to the king

ARABIAN EMPIRE

The stories of the *Arabian Nights* did not come from any one country – many originated in Persia (present-day Iran) and other Middle Eastern countries, and some came from India and China. From about the 7th century, when these stories were being told, most of these countries were linked by a vast empire – the Islamic empire, and many shared a common language (Arabic), a common faith (Islam), and a common way of life.

Where the stories came from
This map shows the area that the *Arabian Nights* stories came from. The Islamic empire extended from Morocco in northwest Africa, stretching across to northern India in the east.

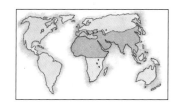

The Ka'ba shrine, Mecca

GROWTH OF ISLAM

Mohammed, the founder of the Islamic religion, was born in Mecca, in present-day Saudi Arabia, in AD 570. At this time, the Arab peoples worshipped many gods, but Mohammed preached about one God – Allah. His following grew quickly – most of the Arab people were very poor and they were attracted to Islam because they felt its teachings offered them the chance of a fairer society.

Spread of Islam
After Mohammed's death in 632, Muslim armies began to spread Islam throughout the Middle East, and into parts of Europe and India. Most of the conquered peoples became Muslims, and Arabic

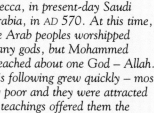

Muslims pray facing Mecca.

became the most important language. Islam was central to people's life – Muslims prayed five times a day, as they still do today. In the *Arabian Nights* tales, the characters often praise Allah or ask him for guidance.

The Koran
The Koran is the holy book of Islam. Muslims believe the Koran was revealed by God to his prophet, Mohammed, in the Arabian Desert in the 7th century. Muslims treat the Koran with great respect, and wash before touching it.

Page from the Koran

Mosque lamp

Islamic art
Muslim artists created intricate geometric designs, decorating books, carpets, and pottery. The designs did not portray any living things, because of the belief that nothing should be worshipped apart from Allah, and that Allah is the only creator of life.

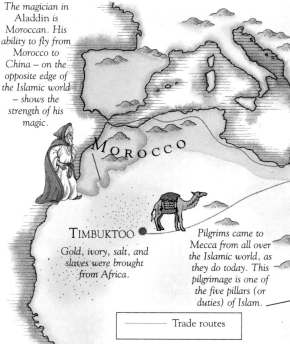

The magician in Aladdin is Moroccan. His ability to fly from Morocco to China – on the opposite edge of the Islamic world – shows the strength of his magic.

MOROCCO

TIMBUKTOO
Gold, ivory, salt, and slaves were brought from Africa.

Pilgrims came to Mecca from all over the Islamic world, as they do today. This pilgrimage is one of the five pillars (or duties) of Islam.

——— Trade routes

AFRICA

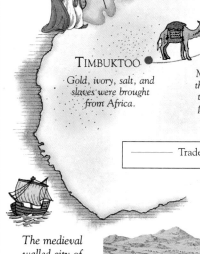

The medieval walled city of Baghdad

Baghdad
The magnificent medieval city of Baghdad was the capital of the Islamic empire and its cultural centre. Great advances in mathematics, science, philosophy, and medicine were made here, and the city had more than 1,000 doctors and many specialist hospitals. The caliph, or ruler, Harun al-Rashid (see box, right) liked to disguise himself and roam among his people in the city's busy, narrow streets – and he appears in this role in *The Garden of Enchantments*. Today, Baghdad is the capital of Iraq.

Trade links

The powerful Islamic empire was a centre for trade, and several major trade routes passed through its lands. As a result, the Arabic language spread and was spoken by many different peoples. This made communications easier, and led to the *Arabian Nights* stories being passed on by word of mouth across a vast area.

Arab merchants travelled by ship to India, Sri Lanka, and China.

Merchants and travellers journeyed by camel caravan or on horseback along land routes, such as the Silk Road, bringing back a huge variety of goods, such as silks, pottery, and spices.

Through Baghdad passed Chinese porcelain, African gold, and Egyptian grain.

In ancient times, Persia had been the centre of a powerful empire. It then merged with the Islamic empire, but retained its language and literary traditions.

Although China remained separate from the Islamic empire, and retained its own religions and way of life, trading links opened up communications between the two cultures.

The Tale of Shahrazad is set in Persia (Iran).

BEIJING

The Silk Road

CHINA

BAGHDAD

PERSIA

CAIRO

Aladdin is set mainly in China.

ARABIA

Ali Baba

Farizad in The Garden of Enchantments journeys into India. Much of the northwest of India became part of the Islamic empire in the 1400s, and many Muslims settled here.

INDIA

Ali Baba and The Fisherman and the Jinnee are Arabic stories about ordinary people who encounter magic.

MECCA

Sandalwood, ebony, and rubies were brought from India.

The fisherman

SRI LANKA

N

A FLOURISHING CULTURE

Mohammed had established a new religion and a new society. Islamic beliefs were expressed in government, the arts, business, and in everyday life. People from different countries and different backgrounds became united under the Islamic faith and the Arabic language. At the end of the 8th century, Islamic civilization reached its height under the rule of Harun al-Rashid. People were wealthier, better educated, and lived more comfortably than people in medieval Europe. It was in this climate that the Arabian Nights tales flourished.

The story-loving caliph

Harun al-Rashid (766–809) was a learned ruler. He encouraged art, poetry, music, and literature – and he loved to hear stories. The storytellers of his court in Baghdad flattered the king by making him the hero of several of their tales, and his court was the setting for many stories told in the *Arabian Nights*.

KEY DATES OF THE ISLAMIC EMPIRE

- **AD 622** Mohammed, prophet and leader of the Islamic people, founds the Muslim state at Mecca, which expands during the next 200 years.
- **673** The Islamic army is driven away from Europe after besieging the largest European city, Constantinople (present-day Istanbul).
- **750** The descendants of Mohammed – the Abbasid Caliphate – rule the Islamic world.
- **786–809** Harun al-Rashid rules the empire at its cultural peak from Baghdad.
- **c1350** The Islamic empire starts its decline.

ARABIAN DAYS

Although many stories from the *Arabian Nights* contain magic, they are firmly rooted in the daily life of medieval Islamic culture, in all its richness and variety. The *Nights* include stories about lowly fishermen, woodcutters, robbers, and slave girls – as well as tales of wealthy kings and beautiful princesses.

FAMILY LIFE

The family was central to Islamic life. People lived quietly and privately in close family groups, bonded by a deep sense of responsibility and duty. Family loyalty and rivalry are central themes in many of the tales. In The Garden of Enchantments, Farizad shows her devotion to her two brothers, whereas in Ali Baba, Kasim is envious of his brother.

Learning a trade

Trades were usually passed from father to son for generation after generation. In early written versions of *Aladdin*, the boy's father is a tailor by trade. Before he dies, he tries to teach Aladdin his skills, but the boy is too lazy to learn.

A tailor in his workshop

Life in the home

Houses were simply furnished. People ate sitting on cushions on the floor, gathered round a selection of foods. Curtains were hung between rooms as partitions.

Slavery

Slaves were relatively well treated and often lived as part of the family, like Marjana in *Ali Baba*. Some were well educated and became government officials or soldiers. Islam laid down rules for the humane treatment of slaves and servants, allowing them to own property, and embarked on abolishing slavery.

Persian slave girl

At the souk

All of life was found in the souk, or market, which lay at the heart of an Islamic town. Here traders gathered to sell all sorts of goods, including silks, spices, herbal medicines, carpets, and jewellery. Along the narrow streets lined with shops and stalls, passers by would stop to browse, haggle, and exchange news.

In the centre of the town stood the mosque, its minaret rising above the bustling market streets.

Minaret

Coffee house

Men gathered at the coffee house to drink, smoke, and chat, or to relax and be entertained by storytellers and street performers, such as acrobats, musicians, and dancers. In places such as this, stories from the *Arabian Nights* would have first been told.

Storyteller

Men smoked pipes called hubble-bubbles; the smoke was drawn into the mouth through a long tube.

Fishermen, lik the one in Th Fisherman and Jinnee, would b their catch of fisl the souk to sel

From the mosque's minaret the muezzin, or crier, would call Muslims to prayer five times a day.

Flat dwelling

Houses were made of sun-baked mud bricks and had flat roofs. These roofs were useful – people could dry their clothes and fruit and grain on them, and in hot weather they might choose to sleep out on the roof.

Food

Stalls piled high with fragrant spices, including cinnamon, cumin, ginger, and coriander, jostled for space alongside stalls selling dried fruits, savoury dishes, and sweet snacks, such as baklavas – pastries layered with nuts.

Dried apricots

Dates

Delicate pastries were stuffed with dates or nuts.

Cinnamon

Dried rose petals were used to flavour tea, and rose water was used to perfume sweets.

Saffron

Women carried jars of grain, dried fruit, or water on their heads.

Water-carrier

Crime

Pickpockets and thieves, working alone or in organized groups, were commonplace in busy markets. They relied on cunning, rather than violence, to steal from passers by.

A young pickpocket steals from a wealthy merchant.

Woodcutters, like Ali Baba, often used donkeys to carry their wood to market to sell; people depended on wood for making fires for cooking and heating.

POSITION OF WOMEN

In the Arabian Nights, women are sometimes described in a romantic, idealistic way, but they are also often shown to be strong and wise: the characters of Shahrazad, Marjana, and Farizad are all very resourceful. Under Islamic law, although women were not treated as equal to men, they were better off than they had been under traditional Arab law. According to the Koran, women were allowed a share in family inheritances and could own property. However, it was the man of the house who had authority over his wife, children, and other relatives.

Women always wore a veil in public.

Rich women waited on by a slave girl.

Wealthy women

Wealthy women were often well educated and well read, like Shahrazad. They might be artists, writers, or supporters of the arts. They had servants to look after them, and they dressed in fine clothes of silks and muslin, and wore elaborate jewellery.

Women's work

Many women spent much of their time at home – looking after the children, cooking food, baking bread, keeping the house clean and tidy, and making daily trips to the well to fetch drinking water. Some women earned money by spinning and weaving clothes – as Aladdin's mother did. Slave girls like Marjana lived in the home and helped with all the household tasks. They sometimes entertained guests by dancing and singing.

Marjana dancing in Ali Baba and the Forty Thieves.

Tales from the *Arabian Nights* are traditionally told within this "frame" story, which features the clever and wise heroine, Shahrazad.

Kerbala mosque, Iraq
Arabian wonder
The opulent palaces and domed mosques of the Islamic empire make a fabulous setting for this royal tale.

Harun al-Rashid in his court
Wise ruler
The finer qualities of King Shahryar call to mind Harun al-Rashid. Unlike Shahryar, however, Harun was a wise ruler who would never have made such an evil vow.

THE TALE
of
QUEEN SHAHRAZAD

LONG AGO, in a far-away land of blue skies, yellow deserts, and white marble palaces, there lived a king with a broken heart. This king's name was Shahryar: he was noble and handsome and once he had been very happy. But his wife had a terrible secret; for though she pretended to care for the king, really she was in love with one of their worthless servants. One day, when this ill-matched pair were meeting in a shadowy corner of the palace, the king happened to stumble upon them, and caught his queen laughing shamelessly as the servant clasped her in his arms.

With a terrible cry, King Shahryar pulled out his sword.

Shahryar was devastated. With a terrible cry, he pulled out his sword and chopped off both their heads.

Then he crept wretchedly back to his rooms.

A short time later, a horse drew up outside; and in walked his brother, Shahzaman, who had just ridden from his own kingdom, over the distant mountains.

"My dear brother," Shahzaman cried, "whatever is the matter?"

In a trembling voice, Shahryar told him everything.

"But this is unbelievable!" exclaimed Shahzaman, "for just before

I left home, almost exactly the same thing happened to me!" And he told Shahryar how he had caught his own wife kissing one of their servants, and how he too had lost his temper and cut off her head.

Then the two kings wept and raged together, wailing that women were the wickedest of creatures, and could never be trusted again.

Shahzaman returned home, leaving King Shahryar to stare into the misty waters of his fountain. At last he made a terrible vow.

"Tomorrow night I shall marry a new wife, but I will not allow her to enjoy being queen. For as soon as the morning dawns I shall have her executed. The next night, and the next morning, I shall do the same with another bride. And then another, and another, and another, until every woman in my kingdom is dead!"

Betrayal

In Islamic culture, men were the head of the household. While it was wrong for a man to betray his wife – it was a far graver wrong for a woman to betray her husband. King Shahryar is deeply insulted because of his wife's deception and because she was with someone of low rank – a mere servant.

The two kings wept and raged together.

The king was enthralled by Shahrazad's rich tapestry of adventure, romance, and magic.

Clever woman
The early versions of the Arabian Nights *say that Shahrazad (pronounced Sha-ha-ra-zad) was witty, wise, and eloquent. She had read countless stories, legends, and poems, and had studied philosophy, the arts, and the sciences.*

And so it was. Every night, King Shahryar chose a new bride, and every morning the poor woman would be executed, until the kingdom grew weak with the terror of it.

Many people fled with their daughters to other kingdoms, until at last, there was only one possible bride left. She was no ordinary girl, for her father was the king's chief minister. Her name was Shahrazad.

The chief minister's heart was filled with dread and sorrow when he was told to condemn his own beloved daughter to death. But Shahrazad refused to share his dismay. She was wiser and cleverer than all the other girls, and together with her younger sister, she made a careful plan and refused to feel afraid.

As soon as the short wedding ceremony was over, Shahryar led Shahrazad to his chamber. But before he could lock the door, a terrible wailing started up outside.

"Oh your Majesty," said Shahrazad, "that must be my little sister, Dunyazad. She is crying for her usual bedtime story. As this is the

14

very last night I will be alive to tell it to her, please, *please* may she come in?"

Before Shahryar could say "no", she opened the door, pulled Dunyazad inside, sat her down and began: "There was once an evil magician …"

Shahryar almost exploded with anger. He tried to spoil the story by ranting and raging; but the sisters just ignored him. At last he sat down with a sigh – and soon found himself enthralled by Shahrazad's rich tapestry of adventure, romance, and magic. Little Dunyazad curled up on the carpet and fell asleep, but the king continued to listen. Then suddenly – at the most exciting moment in the tale – Shahrazad stopped.

"Continue!" commanded the king.

"But dawn is breaking," said Shahrazad, "and I can hear the executioner sharpening his sword."

"Well, he will have to wait!" exclaimed the king. "As soon as I have had a little nap, I order you to finish this tale. I must know what happens next!"

The king slept long and deeply. He awoke at dusk and made Shahrazad finish her story. But when it was done, he was still not satisfied. "Tell me another!" he demanded.

So Shahrazad smiled and began again:

"There was once …"

Again, it was not finished when morning came and it was time for her to die; again, the king was desperate to hear its end. So he let Shahrazad live to finish telling it; and when this was done, he made her start another story straight away. And so it went on.

Now the king was constantly on tenterhooks, waiting to know what would happen next, or what shape her next story might take. All day he slept peacefully, dreaming of the golden pictures she conjured into his mind: and all night long he sat up entranced, listening to the music of her words.

Vizier
An Arabic king's chief minister was known as a vizier. He was head of administration and advised the king on court affairs, but the king's word was law, as Shahrazad's father knows only too well.

Storytelling in a courtyard

Art of storytelling
Shahrazad, like a true storyteller, knows how to keep her audience captivated. She cunningly waits until dawn before reaching the climax of her story – knowing the king will want to hear more.

Dunyazad carried twin babies, and a tiny boy came crawling behind her.

Wedding feast
King Shahryar marries Shahrazad a second time to symbolize his change of heart. After a simple wedding service, the couples would have enjoyed lavish celebrations, and been entertained by slave girls dancing and making music.

Thus days passed, weeks passed, months passed, years passed; and with them, strange things happened. Shahrazad grew fat and then became suddenly thin. Twice she disappeared for nights on end then came back without an explanation. The king did not ask any questions.

One morning, Shahrazad ended a tale just as dawn was breaking and said, "There: I am quite finished. I have no more stories to tell you. Do you realize Shahryar, that one-thousand-and-one whole nights have passed since we were married! But listen, someone is knocking at the door. It must be the executioner. At last you can send me out to him."

But instead of the executioner, in came Dunyazad – who had grown up into a beautiful young woman herself. In her arms she was carrying twin babies, and a tiny boy came crawling along behind her.

"My dear husband," said Shahrazad smiling, "before you behead me, I must introduce you to my children. *Our* children. For in the three years since we were married, I have borne you three sons – but you were too engrossed in my stories to realize."

At these words, Shahryar looked into his own heart – and found it suddenly flooded with sunshine. He gazed at his children and felt a rush of love. Then he turned to Shahrazad, and realized that he could never have her killed now, for he himself could not live without her.

So he sent the executioner away for good.

The king dispatched messengers to his brother, Shahzaman, describing all that had happened, and urging him to come and marry Dunyazad without delay. Shahzaman did, and they had a magnificent double wedding.

And so the two kings and two queens reigned peacefully over their two kingdoms, and lived long and happy lives.

As for the stories, Shahryar and Shahzaman begged Shahrazad

to tell them all over again: the tales of Aladdin, Ali Baba, The Garden of Enchantments, the Fisherman and the Jinnee, and many, many more.

And ever since that time, they have never been forgotten.

1,001 Nights
Shahrazad's name means "born in a city". Her cleverness saved not only herself but the whole kingdom from the king's tyranny. The stories she tells make up the Arabian Nights, *or the* Thousand and One Nights. *This does not mean Shahrazad told exactly 1,001 tales – in Arabic, 1,001 represents a large amount.*

The two couples celebrated with a magnificent double wedding.

17

ALADDIN
and the
WONDERFUL LAMP

The magician mixed a brew of many-coloured magic powders.

Arabic storytellers chose to set *Aladdin* in a far away land – China – to add mystery and romance to the tale. However, many of the story's features remain essentially Arabic.

Divination

Morocco, in North Africa, was famed for sorcery throughout the Islamic world. African magicians used potions, powders (such as those shown below), and other tools to find out, or divine, the unknown.

Lovage root

Orris root

Divination tool
This bowl was filled with sand and hit with a stick; the pattern formed was then interpreted.

THERE WAS ONCE an evil magician from Morocco who longed to gain power over all the treasure in the world.

One night, when the darkness lay deepest, this magician squatted in his lair, mixing many-coloured magic powders; then he sprinkled them on the floor and touched them with a flame. Soon they caught light and burnt into an acrid, swirling mist, shimmering and shifting endlessly into flickering shapes of faces, landscapes, and jewels. Now he chanted the words of hideous spells over them. Slowly, softly, the mist fell still and fixed itself into a vision.

Within it, the magician saw at last all the secrets he longed to know. He saw, on the far side of the world, the exotic land of China. He saw a towering mountain, and within its slopes the shape of a great stone slab, in the middle of which was a gleaming copper ring. He divined that this slab was like a door, behind which lay unimaginable riches; but that door could never be opened except by one unique person: a boy, who bore the name *Aladdin*.

At this discovery, the magician wasted no time. He turned himself into a shadow-bird. Then he flew across oceans and plains, forests, mountains, and deserts, far, far towards the East, until he arrived in China. Disguising himself as an ordinary man, he wandered through that country, asking at every village, town, and city he came to, if anyone knew Aladdin.

At first, he had no success. But then at last, in the emperor's own city, people began to smile and nod at the name, and pointed him towards a market-place. There, amongst the bales of silk and fragrant sacks of spices, he heard voices calling the very name he longed to hear:

"Aladdin, you good-for-nothing wretch!" they shouted. "Get out of here, you trouble-maker!"

And then a young boy came laughing and racing through the narrow passages between the stalls – straight into the magician's outstretched arms.

Aladdin
In many versions of the story, Aladdin is described as a lazy, good-for-nothing boy of 15. He would rather play with his friends in the streets than learn a trade.

A young boy came racing through the market stalls.

The sun setting on Mount Huangshan in eastern China.

Mystical place
Mountains were believed to be mystical places, and made ideal settings for magical happenings.

"So!" cried the magician, "Aladdin – the very person I was looking for!"

The boy jumped back like a nervous rabbit.

"Who are you?" he whispered.

The magician's face twisted into a grin. "My dear boy, don't you know me? I am your long lost uncle. I have travelled thousands of miles right across the world to find you – and to help you."

Aladdin tried to edge away; but the magician seized his arm. "Don't be afraid," he simpered. "My poor Aladdin: I know all about you. I know that your father (my own dear brother) is dead; I know that you and your old mother have no money and often go hungry. That is why I have come to take you away – to make you rich!"

With these words, he whirled Aladdin firmly around and marched him out of the market-place. Aladdin yelled and

The magician chanted into the billowing smoke

An enormous hole opened up into the mountain.

struggled, but it made no difference: the magician hurried him out of the city, through the countryside and into the wilderness. On and on they went. The magician's grip was like iron, and he would not let go. At sunset they came to a great mountain that loomed darkly out of the lonely plain; and there they stopped.

Aladdin watched fearfully as the magician gathered a pile of sweet-smelling twigs and set fire to it, chanting weirdly into the billowing smoke, and throwing incense into the flames. All at once there was a deafening clap of thunder. The ground shook. Then an enormous hole opened up into the mountain. Wedged inside it was a heavy stone slab. In the centre of the slab was a gleaming copper ring.

"Aladdin," hissed the magician, "lift that slab and enter the mountain! Inside you will find a cave. Do not touch anything there, but walk straight through until you come into an enchanted garden. There you will see a stone pedestal, and on top of this a small lamp. Pick the lamp up carefully and bring it back to me."

"But … "

The magician pulled out a ring and slipped it onto Aladdin's finger. "Here, I will let you borrow this. It will protect you from danger while you are underground."

Incense was often used in religious rites, and was burnt in containers like this Syrian incense burner made of silver and gold.

Incense crystals

Burning incense
The fragrant smoke produced from burning incense was believed to carry wishes up to heaven, but the magician uses it for a less godly purpose.

Silver Islamic ring

Magic ring
The magician is so desperate to get Aladdin into the cave, he rashly gives him his personal ring.

Persian painting of people relaxing in a garden.

Peaceful havens

Throughout Asia, gardens represented spiritual peace and harmony, and in the Islamic faith they symbolized Paradise. At night, garden courtyards were lit by candles, and made magical settings for storytelling, music, and courtship. The sparkling glass marbles make the cave garden Paradise on Earth.

The wick was placed in the end hole

Oil was poured into this hole

Magic lamp

Oil lamps were the only source of light in the home and every household had at least one. The lamp that Aladdin finds appears to be like any other lamp.

"But how …?"

"Just do it!" the magician cried, and he pushed Aladdin towards the stone slab. As Aladdin fell against it, the slab opened up, and he found himself stumbling down some steps.

He was in a great, empty cave, as black and cool as night. At first he could see nothing; but then he made out some large shapes here and there, darker than the darkness, glowing strangely at the top. He crept up to one and found that it was an enormous earthenware jar, filled to the brim with gleaming gold coins.

Remembering the magician's warning, he did not dare touch it. Instead he walked slowly on, his heart pounding, towards a distant beam of light.

As he came closer, he saw that this was another opening. He passed through it, and found himself in the Enchanted Garden.

This garden lay in the very heart of the mountain: though it was open to the sky, it was heavily shaded on all sides by sheer walls of craggy, grey rock. Many gnarled trees grew there, each one heavy with fruit. Breathlessly, Aladdin reached out and touched one. He was startled to discover that the plump "fruits" were really sparkling glass marbles, green and red, blue, yellow, purple, and transparent white. He picked some of each kind and stuffed them into his pockets, then hurried on.

At last he came to the stone pedestal. On top of it stood a small brass oil lamp. It looked rather old and very tarnished. Whatever did the magician want it for?

Aladdin picked up the lamp and wrapped it inside his shirt for safety. Then he went back, through the garden and the gold-gleaming cave, then up the steps, until he reached the top and could see daylight above.

The magician was waiting for him.

"Got it, have you?" he screeched. "Then hand it over!" He reached out and tried to snatch the lamp from Aladdin; but it was caught inside the boy's shirt, and the

magician's impatient, grabbing fingers could not reach it.

"Bad boy! How dare you try to keep it from me!" He gave
Aladdin a hard slap. The force of it made Aladdin fall, right
back – into the cave …

The next minute, there was a loud crash, and the heavy stone slab
slammed tightly shut behind him.

*On top of the stone
pedestal stood a small
brass oil lamp.*

Slowly, the smoke
settled and grew until
it took the form of a
fearsome jinnee.

The magician was beside himself with rage. For the stone slab could only be lifted, from the outside, by Aladdin; and he had lost not only the boy, but also the lamp. It was this lamp that contained all the magic powers he had travelled so far to obtain. He cursed and screamed and clawed at his hair like a rabid beast, but there was no way he could undo his mistake. Finally, in a shudder of infernal wings, he flew back across the world to lick his wounds in the darkness of his own lair. And there we must leave him for a while.

Meanwhile, back inside the cave, Aladdin lay bruised and terrified after his fall. He began to panic, for he quickly realized that he was trapped. Perhaps God was punishing him for always being so lazy, cheeky, and good-for-nothing. He imagined how he would have to stay there forever; he imagined what it would be like to die, slowly and painfully, of hunger and thirst. These bleak thoughts made him vow that, if ever he escaped, he would change his ways and do his best to live a useful life. Meanwhile, all he could do now was weep and moan; he writhed about and twisted his hands together. In this way, he inadvertently rubbed the magician's ring.

Now, this ring was a magic one. As soon as it was rubbed, blue smoke came spilling out of it. Slowly, the smoke settled and grew, until it took the solid form of a fearsome jinnee.

"Master," cried the jinnee in a voice that seemed to rumble from the deepest bowels of the earth, "I am the slave of this magic ring. Your wish is my command. Tell me what you want – and I will give it to you at once."

At first, Aladdin could only cower back against the steps, unable to speak. The jinnee waited, glowering. Aladdin whispered, "I … I wish I was … out of this dreadful cave – and safely back in my own home."

Almost before the words were out of his mouth, he was caught up in a dazzling whirlwind of coloured light; his stomach lurched and he seemed to faint. Round and round he spun, on and on, through the never-ending coils of time and space …

By and by, everything grew still. Aladdin opened his eyes.

He was safely back in his own home, with his mother staring at him in utter astonishment.

Jinn

A jinnee (or genie) is a spirit in Arabic folklore. Some jinn are evil and ugly, others are good and beautiful. In the Arabian Nights, jinn often appear out of small objects, such as a ring. Once released they have supernatural powers, but they still have to obey the owner of the object.

Jinn can take the shape of animals (above), monsters, or humans.

Some jinn cause people harm; this man is wrestling with a jinnee.

Evil and powerful jinn are known as *ifreet*.

Chinese woman spinning cotton

Working mother
*Aladdin's mother was
a widow and had to earn
her own living, which was
not easy for a woman in
these times. Early versions
of the story say she worked
at spinning wool and cotton,
a badly paid job done
by women.*

Aladdin's home
*Aladdin and his mother
were poor and their home
would have been simply
furnished. They would have
eaten basic foods, such as
beans and rice, out of simple
wooden or earthenware
dishes. They rarely could
have afforded meat.*

Aladdin's old mother listened in horror and amazement as he told her all about the magician, the cave, the ring, and the jinnee.

When he had finished she shook her head sadly and said, "Oh Aladdin, if only you could do something useful for a change, instead of getting mixed up in such wickedness and danger! Didn't I beg you this morning to go out and earn some money? Well, because you ignored me as usual, we can't afford to buy any food. There's nothing at all left in the house, and no money in my pocket. We will both starve to death!"

Aladdin looked away in shame; and his eye

"I am the slave of the lamp," the jinnee bellowed.

26

fell upon the lamp that he had brought back from the cave.

"Listen, Mother," he said, "why don't I take that old lamp to the market, and see if I can sell it? The magician acted as if it were really valuable. Surely someone will give me some money for it."

"No one will want to buy a filthy old thing like that," she said. "Here, let me polish it up for you." She picked up a rag, spat on it and rubbed it over the lamp.

At once, the lamp began to hum. Then it began to spark and flash. The next minute, in a cloud of purple smoke, out jumped another jinnee, three times bigger and three times mightier than the first one.

"I am the slave of the lamp," he bellowed. "Tell me what you wish for, and I will give it to you."

At the sight of this devilish creature, Aladdin's mother gave a shriek of terror and fainted to the floor. But Aladdin snatched the lamp from her and cried, "We wish for food – and plenty of it!"

In a flash, a huge silver tray appeared on top of the jinnee's head. It was laden with succulent roast meats, fragrant rice, piles of luscious fruits, pastries dripping with honey, and two enormous flasks of rich, red wine. The jinnee set the tray upon a table, and then he vanished.

By this time, the old woman had come to. For a few moments she and Aladdin could do nothing but stare at this feast. Never in their lives had they seen anything like it. Then the delicious smells got the better of them, and they sat down to eat until they both felt ready to burst with contentment. When they had finished, Aladdin stood up. "There's something else I forgot to show you, Mother," he said; and from his pockets he pulled out the coloured marbles he had found in the Enchanted Garden.

Aladdin and his mother stared at the delicious feast.

Chinese silverware, c800s

Silver jug used for holding water or wine

Stemmed cup

Silver dish

Gilded silver tray

Silver service
The jinnee presented Aladdin and his mother with a feast laid out on silverware. China was known throughout the Islamic empire for its fine metalwork. The Chinese traded gold and silver as well as silks, spices, and paper with Middle Eastern countries via the Silk Road.

Precious gems

Aladdin's realization of the gems' true worth marks his growth from an innocent boy to a mature, worldly-wise young man.

Diamond

Ruby

Sapphire

Emerald

Bathing beauty

The princess visits the hammam, *an Islamic bath house. There were separate bath houses for men and women. Women went to the* hammam *to meet other women and to cleanse and beautify themselves.*

Behind the veil

The Princess Badr al-Budur (her name means full moon of full moons), hides her beauty behind a veil. In accordance with Islamic law, veils are traditionally worn by Muslim women as a sign of modesty.

Aladdin's mother gasped. She took the marbles from him one by one, and held them in the palm of her wrinkled old hand. Then she hobbled to the door and held each one up, so that a rainbow-light danced out of it.

"Oh Aladdin," she exclaimed, "you are the most ignorant of boys! These are not marbles – they are jewels! These glowing ones are rubies, sapphires, and emeralds; and this one that seems to shimmer with fire, is a real diamond! We are rich, Aladdin! We are rich!"

From that moment, life changed completely for Aladdin and his mother, for the jewels were worth a fortune. They sold enough to buy themselves a fine new house, filled with delicately carved furniture, and staffed with many attentive servants. They both began to dress in richly coloured silk, and thanks to the jinnee of the lamp, they always dined on the most delicious food.

In this way, the years passed quickly; and Aladdin grew up from a naive boy into a handsome, bold young man.

One day when he was walking through the city, he came upon a magnificent procession, taking the emperor's daughter, Princess Badr al-Budur to the baths. At the head of this procession there marched a pair of heralds, who loudly commanded every inhabitant of the city to hide indoors as they passed; for it was forbidden upon pain of death for any common person to gaze upon the princess's beauty.

However, Aladdin was emboldened by all his adventures. He decided to risk his life and disobey.

He stole secretly through the streets to the very bath house door, and there he was rewarded by a single glimpse of the lovely dark-eyed lady, peeping shyly from behind the embroidered folds of her veil. He fell instantly and passionately in love with her, and knew he could not rest until he had made her his wife.

Aladdin wasted no time: the very next day he sought an audience with the emperor himself, and begged him for his daughter's hand in marriage.

The emperor was so impressed by Aladdin's extraordinary wealth, that he agreed to let him marry the princess. A wonderful wedding feast was held. Afterwards, Aladdin commanded the jinnee of the lamp to conjure up a magnificent gilded palace for them to live in.

However, despite his good fortune, Aladdin did not forget that once he had been very poor. He found many ways to help the city's beggars and needy people, so that he was soon loved and admired by all around him. Thus things worked out for him very well indeed.

But what about the evil magician?

He had certainly not forgotten Aladdin, and through his weird spells he had watched all the good things that had happened to him. He grew mad with jealousy, and determined to get his revenge.

Aladdin was rewarded by a single glimpse of the lovely dark-eyed lady.

*"New lamps for old!
New lamps for old!"
cried the magician.*

Pedlars
*A pedlar was a travelling
salesman who walked through
a town or city shouting out
his wares. The pedlar would
sometimes exchange as well
as sell goods, but here the
magician is offering people
a very good deal.*

The magician flew back to China. There he lay low, lurking in the shadowy fringes of the emperor's city, feeding on rumours, until he heard that Aladdin was away on a hunt, leaving Princess Badr al-Budur alone in their palace. Then he came out of hiding, disguised himself as a pedlar, and went trudging through the streets around the palace, shouting,

"Lamps for sale! New lamps for old! Give me your old lamp, and get a new one in return! New lamps for old!"

It so happened that the princess was taking a walk in the palace garden at that time, and when the disguised magician came past, she heard him shouting on the other side of the wall. At once she thought of the filthy old lamp that Aladdin kept locked away in a box. "I can't imagine why Aladdin has kept that nasty old bit of rubbish for so long," she said to herself. "Well, this is an excellent chance to get rid of it."

Very soon, the magician came knocking at the palace gate. Behind him came a jostling, ragamuffinly crowd of street children, all giggling as they mimicked his outrageous offer: "New lamps for old!" The princess called one of her servants, gave the boy the magic lamp and told him to exchange it at once for a new one.

When the servant opened the door and thrust the magic lamp towards him, the magician could hardly believe his luck. With a crash, he dropped the whole basket of twenty sparkling new lamps at his feet, and greedily snatched the magic lamp from the boy.

Then, throwing off his followers, he scuttled away as fast as he could, into the maze of alleyways of the city, on and on, until he was concealed in a dank passageway where only rats might spy on him. There he stopped and threw off his disguise.

With trembling hands, he held the lamp out before him. "At last," he muttered, "at last!" He began to caress it, with such tenderness that it must surely have been the only thing in all his murky life that he had ever loved.

The lamp began to hum. It sparked and flashed. Purple smoke spilt out of it. And then its jinnee appeared.

"Tell me your wish, oh Master, and I will give it
to you!"

"Take away Aladdin's palace," hissed the magician. "Take also
everything that belongs with it, including the lovely Princess Badr
al-Budur. Carry them straight back to my own country and take
me there too!"

In a brilliant flash of light, the jinnee instantly obeyed.

*The magician greedily
snatched the magic lamp
from the boy.*

31

"You are nothing but an evil trickster – an imposter and a sorcerer!" the emperor cried.

Later that day, the emperor happened to glance out of his window and saw that where Aladdin's palace had been, there was now nothing but an empty space. In a panic, he sent out messengers to discover what had happened to it, but though they searched high and low and questioned thousands of people, they could not discover the cause of this dreadful calamity.

The emperor was beside himself with anger and grief over the disappearance of his beloved daughter. He puzzled and brooded on it, and sought the advice of all his wisest counsellors. He came to the conclusion that Aladdin must be entirely to blame.

By and by, Aladdin returned to the city. As he passed through its golden gates, he was astonished to be seized by fierce guards. They bound him in chains, dragged him straight to the emperor, and hurled him at the mighty one's feet.

"You are nothing but an evil trickster!" the emperor raged at him, "an imposter and a sorcerer! I realize now, that fancy palace of yours was a mere conjuring trick to enable you to steal my daughter. Now it has vanished

into thin air – and so has she. Oh, my poor girl, who is more precious to me than all the jewels in China! What have you done with her, you villain?"

When he heard these words, Aladdin's heart turned icy cold with dismay. He guessed at once that the evil magician was responsible. He tried to explain, but the emperor refused to listen to him. Instead, he commanded his guards to throw Aladdin into prison.

It wasn't long before the people of the city heard what had happened. They came crowding round the royal palace, shouting that Aladdin was their hero and must surely be innocent of any crime. But the emperor had made his decision, and he stonily condemned Aladdin to death.

Aladdin's prison cell was an unlit, airless dungeon where he was fed upon mouldy crusts of bread and muddy water. The emperor allowed him to have no visitors, and no hope.

Then, just as he was about to give in to total despair, Aladdin suddenly remembered that he was still wearing the magician's magic ring; and that once before, when he had been locked away expecting to die, it had saved his life. Now, in the gloom, he felt for it upon his finger and rubbed it.

At once the jinnee appeared:

"Tell me your wish, oh Master, and I shall give it to you."

"Bring me back my palace, oh jinnee," cried Aladdin, "and above all – bring me back my wife!"

But the jinnee shook his head. "Master," he replied hoarsely, "I am sorry. I cannot grant this wish. For your palace and your wife have been stolen by the jinnee of the lamp; and in all truth that jinnee's magic is stronger than any spells of mine. I do not have enough power to undo his work."

Chinese emperor
This story is set in a time when China was a great empire ruled by powerful emperors. Although advice would be sought from counsellors, the emperor's word was final. People who acted against the emperor risked the executioner's sword.

Aladdin and Badr
al-Budur hugged
each other with joy.

**Chinese
jewellery**

Gold
armlet

Gilded silver
comb

Sleeve
weights were
used to weigh
down sleeves
of robes.

Decorative
hairpins, made
of gold and
silver.

Chinese beauty

*Chinese women were famed
for their graceful beauty.
Wealthy women wore
flowing silk robes in vibrant
colours, and stunning
jewellery made from gold or
silver. Their hair was combed
and twisted into elaborate
styles and held in place by
ornate combs and hairpins.*

Desperately, Aladdin tried to think what to do.
"Then take me to the palace!" he cried.

There was a flash of light and the next moment, Aladdin
found himself standing in the magnificent entrance hall of his
own lost palace.

He did not linger there, but went hurrying through
the golden corridors, searching for Princess Badr al-Budur.
He found her before long, safe but very frightened: for the
evil magician had been bullying her to forget Aladdin and
marry him instead; and the more she refused, the angrier
the magician got.

Aladdin and Badr al-Budur hugged and kissed each other in
great joy; and then Aladdin said, "Listen my love, for I have a plan
that I hope will allow us to escape and destroy the magician."

He called up the jinnee of the ring again, commanding it to bring
him a bag of sleeping herbs. At Aladdin's bidding, the princess
dressed in her finest robes, while her maids styled her black hair and
sprayed her with exotic perfume. Then Aladdin hid behind a screen,
and they both waited.

Night fell. The magician came to torment the princess as usual;
but this time she did not cry. Instead, she smiled enticingly and
offered the magician a goblet of wine. He took it and drank it
greedily, not realizing that Aladdin had laced it with sleeping herbs!
Almost at once, the magician tumbled over, and fell into a deep,
deep sleep.

Aladdin leapt from behind the screen, tore open the magician's
robe, and snatched out the magic lamp, which the evil one had kept
hidden there.

Then Aladdin called up the jinnee of the lamp and commanded it
to carry the palace and everything in it straight back to China.

And so it was done.

Aladdin and the princess were relieved and delighted to be safely
back at home together, and the emperor and Aladdin's mother were
extremely glad to see them. When the emperor saw the magician
(still fast asleep) and heard all about his evil deeds, he apologized
to Aladdin from the depths of his heart. Then he ordered his guards

to take the magician away, burn him on a pile of dung, and scatter his ashes in the city's sewage pits.

After that there was no more trouble. The emperor made friends with Aladdin's mother, and together they showered the young couple with blessings. As the years went by, many beautiful children were born to Aladdin and Badr al-Budur, and when the emperor died, Aladdin inherited his throne.

Chinese silver drinking cup

Sleeping potion
The princess tricks the magician into taking the sleeping potion, by pretending she is in love with him.

The princess offered the magician a glass of wine.

This Persian story features a typical quest. The innocent heroine must overcome many difficulties as she searches for the magic objects that will bring her happiness.

The king heard three sisters chatting together.

Master of disguises
The king in this story is based on Harun al-Rashid, who used to wander through the streets of Baghdad disguised as a merchant to hear what people were saying about him and his state.

THE
GARDEN
OF ENCHANTMENTS

THERE WAS ONCE a king of Persia who liked to disguise himself as a common man, and wander secretly through the humblest streets and alleyways of his kingdom.

One night he came to a quarter of the city where he had never been before. There he heard young women's voices, and stopped to listen by an open door that led into a cramped and gloomy house.

The first voice said, "How I wish I were married to the king's pastrycook! Then instead of having to slave all day, I could lie around and feast on my husband's delicious pastries."

The second said, "Suit yourself, sister. I prefer mouthwatering savouries, so I'll claim the king's chef as my husband."

The king cupped his ear and crept closer. He heard the women giggling together; and then a third voice whispered, "Oh my sisters, you are welcome to all that food. This is *my* heart's desire: I long only to be blessed with such goodness that I might be chosen to marry the king."

When the king heard this, he smiled softly. "There is no finer deed one can do," thought he, "than to make a poor person happy – and to help three at once is even better!" Thus he resolved that, the very next day, he would make each of the sisters' wishes come true.

And so the three young women each married their chosen husbands. But while the youngest was full of happiness, and was honoured with fine jewels and beautiful dresses, the other two had only food to delight them. Within weeks of the weddings, the two older women were smitten by the creeping darkness of jealousy. They grew to hate their youngest sister, simply because she was now the queen.

The months passed and soon the queen gave birth to a beautiful baby boy. But before she had even seen him, her jealous sisters snatched the child away, laid him in a willow basket, and put it to float on the river. Then they took a dead puppy to the king, telling him that his wife had given birth to that.

The king was horror-struck, the queen was heartbroken, but life went on, and soon she gave birth to another lovely son. But just as the last time, her sisters snatched him away, set him afloat upon the river, and presented the king with a dead kitten as his child.

There was more sorrow and more anguish; but the moon continued to wax and wane until the queen gave birth for the third time. Now it was a pretty daughter that the wicked sisters seized and set adrift upon the river, and a dead mouse that they presented to the king.

At last the king felt he could not take any more of this ill-omened marriage. Sadly, he had his unfortunate wife taken away and locked up all alone in a forgotten room in a cold, silent corner of the palace. The two heartless sisters were beside themselves with joy.

Mouthwatering food

Many ordinary people could not afford to eat well, so to feast on tasty foods, like the two elder sisters desire, would be a favourite fantasy.

Baklava, a delicious Arabic sweet made from pastry and nuts.

Childbirth

It was a deep-rooted belief amongst women that if they committed a sin, Allah might punish them by making them give birth to a deformed baby or creature.

Before the queen could even hold her baby boy, her jealous sisters snatched the child away.

But out of this darkness, a small light gleamed and slowly grew. For the queen's three stolen babies did not die. Instead the river carried each one gently downstream to lodge amongst the whispering reeds; and there each was found in turn by the king's own gardener.

This gardener and his wife had no children of their own, so they welcomed the three abandoned babies with all the love they could find. They called the eldest boy Farid, the second boy Faruz, and the girl Farizad.

Having no idea that these were really the king's children, they brought them up in their own way, with wisdom and simplicity, until they were fully grown. Then the gardener retired, and the king gave him his own plot of land, to thank him for his many years of loyal service. Time passed happily and peacefully, until first the wife and then the gardener died, leaving their adopted children their humble house and its very beautiful garden.

One day Farid and Faruz went out hunting, leaving Farizad at home alone. As she sat in the garden, a bent old woman came hobbling along and knocked upon the gate calling,

Each child was found in turn by the king's own gardener.

River babies

This story recalls the biblical tale in which the baby Moses is put in a basket and placed in the bulrushes of the River Nile. Moses' mother did this to protect him from being harmed by the Egyptians. Moses was later found by the pharaoh's daughter, who looked after him.

"Oh dear, how weary I am! I am worn out and dusty, and my throat is parched from the hot desert wind. Who is there that will help me?"

At once, Farizad threw open the gate, took the old crone's gnarled hand, and gently led her into the garden. She took her to a shady tree and refreshed her with cool drinks and a dish of figs. They sat in the warm shadows of the passing afternoon, talking quietly of this and that; and all the while the old woman gazed around with eyes that were night-black, and yet bright as stars.

She said, "My dear, you may think that you have everything you want, but you are wrong. You may believe that this garden is perfect, but three things are missing from it. Until you find them, you can never truly be happy."

"Well!" cried Farizad in surprise, "And what are they?"

The old woman stood up and hobbled back to the gate. There she stopped and smiled secretly to herself.

"I should not tell you," she said, "for once you know of them, you will find no rest until you have won them, and I fear that your quest may end only in waste and tears."

Farizad came after her, and begged to be told.

The old woman took both her hands and held Farizad's eyes with her own star-dark gaze. "Oh, poor girl," she whispered, "what can I do, but let you into this fearful secret? The three things you are missing are: the Talking Bird, the Singing Tree, and the Golden Water. If you wish to find them, you must journey for twenty days until you come to the distant borders of India; and there you will meet a stranger. This man will tell you all you need to know to achieve the desire I have planted in your heart; but be warned, his advice will be difficult to understand, and almost impossible to follow."

Then she dropped Farizad's hands, passed through the gate and disappeared like a dry leaf into the lengthening shadows of evening.

Earthly paradise
In the Islamic faith, striving to achieve a perfect garden symbolized trying to achieve perfection of the soul. Farizad's garden, though beautiful, is incomplete – and this reflects her life.

"My dear," said the old woman, "three things are missing from this garden."

Farid and Faruz returned home at nightfall. They found Farizad pacing round the garden, her eyes bright with excitement. When she told them all that had happened, of the Talking Bird, the Singing Tree, and the Golden Water, they too felt themselves gnawed by a curious longing.

"Whatever these mysterious things are," said Farid, "it seems that now, none of us can rest without them. I am the eldest, so it is my responsibility to go out into the world to search for them. I am not afraid." He took a knife that hung from his belt and gave it to Farizad. "Little sister," he said, "keep this with you and examine it every day. As long as the blade stays clean and bright, you will know that I am well."

Then he mounted his horse, and went galloping off eastwards towards India.

Twenty days passed and twenty nights passed. On the twenty-first morning, Farizad took out Farid's knife and found that its blade was scarred with rust. With a cry of horror, she called Faruz to see it. "Farid must be in trouble," said Faruz. "So I must go after him and save him. Then together we shall continue to search for the Talking Bird, the Singing Tree, and the Golden Water, and bring them home to you."

"No!" replied Farizad, "I beg you Faruz, do not go. This quest has brought nothing but misery since I heard of it, and I cannot bear to lose both my brothers for such a foolish desire."

But Faruz said, "You know as well as I do, that none of us can find any peace until the quest is fulfilled. You cannot stop me, little sister.

Faruz said, "Take this necklace of pearls: as long as they glow bright, all will be well."

Farid said, "Keep this knife with you. As long as the blade stays bright, you will know that I am well."

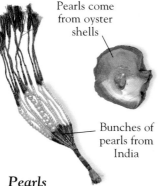

Pearls come from oyster shells

Bunches of pearls from India

Pearls

It was a long-held belief in the East that there was a connection between pearls and their wearers, the one acting upon the other. It was said they went cloudy if the owner was sick, and lost their shine completely if the owner died.

Two medieval Persian warriors

But take this necklace of pearls and look at it each day: as long as they glow bright like this, you can be certain that all is well."

Then he too rode off eastwards towards India.

Twenty more days passed and twenty more nights passed. On the twenty-first morning Farizad took out the necklace and saw that its pearls had turned as dry as bones. Faruz must also be in trouble!

Now she was all alone. She had no brother left to help her, no husband, no father, no uncle. Her heart was burning with sorrow and remorse, for it was her words that had sent Farid and Faruz to their doom.

She knew she had no choice, and that Allah had chosen her path: she must go after them. So she dressed herself as a man, armed herself like a warrior, and mounted her favourite horse. Then she set out after her brothers, on the long, lonely road that led towards the East.

Women warriors

Some women from Islamic countries did go to war, though many more nursed the wounded behind the front line. Aisha, the prophet Mohammed's wife, took part in a war along with other women.

Persian armour

Persian armour was lightweight, so it would have been possible for a woman like Farizad to wear it.

This Persian helmet has a fringe of fine chainmail, and is beautifully inlaid with gold. It would have belonged to a warlord or a nobleman.

Farizad armed herself like a warrior, and mounted her favourite horse.

Holy man
The holy man that Farizad meets would probably have been a Hindu, a member of the main religion in India. A Hindu holy man gives up worldly possessions and seeks enlightenment through meditation and prayer. He offers people advice on how to search for spiritual truths.

Farizad rode through the green wilderness of India for twenty nights and twenty days, meeting no one. On the last day she came to a great tree. Sitting cross-legged beneath it was an old holy man, thin as a skeleton, covered in matted hair, his face radiant with peace.

Farizad climbed from her horse, threw off her hood, and greeted him respectfully. "Saintly uncle," she said, "have you seen my brothers? They came this way not long ago, searching for the Talking Bird, the Singing Tree, and the Golden Water."

"Certainly, I have seen them," the old man nodded. "I have shown each one the path to take. I even gave each a gift to help him, and offered him good advice. But they were just like the hundreds before them who have set out on this quest: they have failed and not returned."

Farizad hesitated. Then she said, "Oh holy man, I have come so far – and I cannot turn back! I must go after my brothers. Please, please help me."

The holy man's expression did not change. He picked up a ball of red granite from the ground and put it into her hands.

"Throw this in front of you, little sister," he said, "and follow where it rolls, up and up to the top of that towering mountain. If only you could reach the summit, you would find the things you long for and be able to free your brothers. But be warned: the path is steep, and as you climb the dangerous voices of the Invisible Ones will come out, to tear at your soul and wrench your heart in two. Do not give in to them, do not listen, do not obey them – otherwise you will be lost like all the others, and turned into stone!"

Wilderness
Farizad's journey up the mountain symbolizes a spiritual search for perfection. The "Invisible Ones" represent worldly distractions she should reject along the way.

Farizad listened carefully and thanked him. Then she took the granite ball from him, and followed where it led her, up the barren slopes of the mountain.

As she climbed, the Invisible Ones began to call to her. At first they were soft but insidious:

"Farizad – look behind you, your brothers are there!"

Then they grew louder, screeching and searing:

"Help, Farizad, for pity's sake! Turn round! Save me!"

Until they tore at the very core of her: *"Farizad, over here – I shall die unless you come!"*

And on and on, ever louder, turning from pleas into shrieks, into screams of utter terror.

Farizad heard them. She longed to turn her head. She yearned to see if her brothers were really there. She ached to think of their suffering. And yet – she remembered the good advice of the holy man. So, struggling with every fibre of her being, she did not stop or turn aside. Steadily she climbed up and on, making herself oblivious to all distraction.

In this way, the voices passed over and around her, vague and harmless as sighs of wind. And at last she emerged past them, through the mists of serenity, to the shining top of the mountain.

Farizad followed the granite ball where it led her, up the barren slopes of the mountain.

43

The good and brave Farizad has resisted all temptation and has reached the mountain top, a symbol of her newly perfect spirit.

Talking Bird
In many cultures, the bird is a symbol of the spirit, and often acts as a messenger. The Talking Bird is a guiding light to Farizad.

Singing Tree
Farizad is rewarded with a musical tree, which represents love and happiness.

A brightly coloured bird was waiting there. As Farizad came close, it opened its beak and spoke:

"Farizad, you have found me! Now I am yours, and I shall do everything you wish."

Farizad's heart was beating fast. "Oh Talking Bird," she cried, "where is the Singing Tree?"

"Behind you," whispered the Bird.

She turned and saw a beautiful, spreading tree.

At that moment, its myriad dancing leaves burst into a shower of music, sweeter than lutes or harps, sweeter even than children's voices.

"Oh Bird," said Farizad, "and where is the Golden Water?"

The Talking Bird stretched its shimmering wings and flew to a turquoise rock. "Come here," it said. She went, and saw that behind the rock a spring gushed endlessly out of the ground, sparkling like gold, yet with the cool, clear taste of mountain water.

Farizad clapped her hands in delight, but still her heart was heavy. Turning back to the Talking Bird she said, "Oh Bird, how can I admire these wonders until I have found my two lost brothers?"

"True enough," said the Talking Bird, fluttering around her. "Now listen, Farizad. First you must break off a single branch of the Singing Tree, ready to carry back to your garden. Then you must go to the Golden Water, take the crystal jar you find there, and fill it from the spring. After that, we will travel down the mountain together. On the way, you must sprinkle drops of Golden Water onto every rock that we pass."

Farizad did as the Talking Bird said. When she was ready, they went down the mountain. Each time they came to a rock, she sprinkled it with Golden Water; and at once, each rock turned into a young man.

Amongst these men were her own lost brothers, Farid and Faruz. They sprang back to life with a cry of pure joy. Then the three of them went down to the foot of the mountain together, and turned towards home.

After twenty days and twenty nights they came happily back to their own garden. There the Talking Bird built its nest, and became

44

the admired king of all the other birds. Farizad planted her branch of the Singing Tree, and within minutes it took root and sprouted into a new Tree, as fine and musical as the first one. Finally, she poured the Golden Water into the basin of their fountain, so that it rose up into a cloud of spray, sparkling like sunshine, yet cool as morning mist.

Never was there a garden filled with such enchantment and beauty! But that was not the end of it.

Golden Water
Water is a universal symbol of life. When Farizad sprinkles water onto the rocks, she gives life back to her brothers, like water in the desert.

Farizad's brothers sprang back to life with a cry of pure joy.

With the Bird, the Tree, and the Water, the garden is complete and symbolizes peace and harmony.

45

One day, the king himself came riding past, having heard many strange rumours of the Garden of Enchantments. He knocked at the gate and was welcomed in by Farid and Faruz.

They refreshed him in the cooling spray of the Golden Water, then led him to a bench under the sweetly humming shade of the Singing Tree. Farizad, meanwhile, went into the kitchen and began to cook stuffed cucumbers, which was the most kingly dish she knew.

As she worked, the Talking Bird flew in and said, "Do not stuff those cucumbers with rice, Farizad: use pearls instead."

"Pearls?" cried Farizad in surprise. But, because she respected the Talking Bird, she did just as it said.

When the dish was ready, she carried it out to the king. He began to eat it with relish – but on the first mouthful he almost choked.

"What is this?" he cried. "Cucumbers stuffed with pearls? Who ever heard of such a thing!"

Poor Farizad flushed with shame. But the Talking Bird flew to sit on the king's plate, cocked its head on one side and said, "Indeed your Majesty, who has heard of such a thing? And indeed, who ever has heard of a queen giving birth to a puppy, a kitten, or a mouse?"

At these words, the king's ancient grief (long buried but always smouldering) welled up like a great volcano. His face darkened and he leaped to his feet. "What is this about?" he exclaimed.

The Talking Bird fluttered gently to Farid's shoulder, "Here is your

The Talking Bird flew to sit on the king's plate.

puppy," it said. Then it flew to Faruz's shoulder, "This one is your kitten." Lastly it came back to Farizad, "And this one is your mouse!

"You had better give thanks to Allah that your wicked sisters-in-law did not kill them, but only sent them away; give thanks that these poor babies did not drown, but were saved and found and rescued by a man whose wisdom is greater than your own!"

The king looked again at Farid, Faruz, and Farizad, and recognized from their faces that they really were his children. Then he looked back at his past and saw that he had been weak, foolish, and cruel.

He took his daughter and two sons into his arms and embraced them in the boundless flood of a father's love. He wept with them and laughed with them, sorrowing for the past but rejoicing for the future.

Then he took his three children back to his palace. There they went at once to the forgotten room where the poor queen had sat alone for twenty long years. They led her out to the bright world, and the king fell to her feet begging for forgiveness. The queen, who was as gentle and good as her sisters were evil, readily welcomed him back into the sunshine of her love; and when she saw her three children not only alive and well but as radiant as three new moons, her happiness knew no bounds. As for her sisters, when they heard the news they fell dead in fits of rage.

But the king and his queen, and their beloved three children, lived happily for many years.

The forty thieves
These forty thieves were highwaymen. They haunted the open road and desert, and waylaid and robbed their victims by brute force.

ALI BABA
and the
FORTY THIEVES

FORTY HORSES CAME GALLOPING through the forest. Crackle. Crackle-crack. CRASH! The horses burst out of the undergrowth and into a clearing. On their backs were forty villainous looking men, with scarred cheeks, black forked beards, and blood-stained daggers dangling from their belts.

"Wha-hoah!"

The forty villains jumped from their horses. They jostled their way to a great, smooth rock that stood at the bottom of a hill. They were all carrying heavy sacks that clinked and jingled as they moved, full of little tears through which came the unmistakable glint of gold.

Their leader was an ogre of a man. He held out his arms towards the rock and cried:

"OPEN, SESAME!"

At once, the rock gaped open like a door. In trooped the forty robbers (for that's what the men were). The darkness swallowed them up. The rock slid shut behind them.

Everything went quiet.

Then there was another, muffled cry of "OPEN, SESAME!", and the rock burst open again. Out came the grinning robbers, dragging their empty sacks. The rock slammed behind them, the robbers jumped on their horses, and then, with a thunder of hooves, they disappeared into the trees.

And that was that. It wasn't the first time this had happened, and it wouldn't be the last.

But this time was different.

Someone had been watching them.

His name was Ali Baba. He was a poor woodcutter, an ordinary, decent sort of fellow; and when he'd heard the robbers coming, he'd left his three old donkeys to graze nearby and scuttled up the nearest tree. Old Ali Baba, he'd seen everything, he'd heard everything. Now he came slithering down from the tree,

Ali Baba left his donkeys to graze.

all wobbly knees and nervously churning belly. He glanced over his shoulder. He stood stock still and listened. He tiptoed to the rock and ran a stubby finger over it. He cleared his throat. "Ahem," he whispered. And then, in a very small voice: "OPEN, SESAME!"

He held out his arms towards the rock and cried: "Open, sesame!"

*The walls were
stacked with
treasure from
floor to ceiling.*

Swiftly, silently, the rock slid
open. Ali Baba hesitated; he swallowed; he
crept in. And then the cave walls closed silently
behind him.

Inside all was dark. Ali Baba's skin turned to goose-pimples.
He crept forward, along a tunnel and into a great cave.
Ali Baba gasped.

The walls were stacked with treasure from floor to ceiling:
gleaming necklaces, caskets filled with gold and silver
bars, bales of silk and brocade velvet, casks of vintage
wine, boxes of sticky sweets, rings and bracelets, brooches
and anklets, silver goblets, bowls, and trophies, piles of
diamonds and precious stones, cascades of wild pearls, sacks full of
gold coins – and lots more.

"I'm not a greedy man," Ali Baba said to himself, "am I? I mean, I never asked Allah to show me into this place, did I? But He knows how poor I am, doesn't He? It's a sign, that's what it is! Allah wants me to help myself to a share of all these riches, I'm sure He does!"

So he grabbed two big bags of gold coins, carried them back to the rock face, whispered the magic words to make the rock slide open, and sneaked out.

Then he called his old donkeys (which had been dozing happily under a tree), loaded the bags of gold onto their panniers, and quickly led them home.

"Oi!" he shouted to his wife. "Come and take a look at what your husband's brought for you!"

She bustled out to see. "Ooh, Ali Baba!" she scolded, "Whoever have you stolen all that gold from?" she cried.

"Just wait till you hear!" he chuckled. By the time he'd finished the story, his wife was jumping with excitement.

Ali Baba wagged a finger at her. "Now remember," he said, " we – must – keep – this – secret."

His wife nodded.

"You know what'll happen if the neighbours find out," Ali Baba went on; "they'll all be wheedling around, wanting a share. So there's no time to lose: we must dig a hole in the kitchen floor and hide the treasure inside."

"Oh, you're so full of good ideas, Ali Baba," she said. "You get right on and start digging. I'll just pop over to your brother Kasim's house to borrow their measure, so we can work out exactly how much gold we've got."

And before Ali Baba could stop her, she rushed next door calling, "Yoo-hoo, anyone at home?"

Kasim's wife was a sour-faced old moaner. "What do you want?" she snorted, coming out to see who it was.

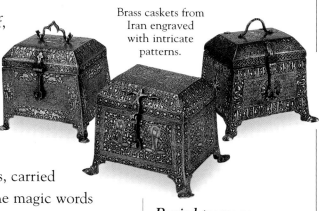

Brass caskets from Iran engraved with intricate patterns.

Buried treasure

As a poor woodcutter, Ali Baba would never have seen such treasures before, and his good fortune reflects the fantasies of many ordinary people. As a Muslim, he believes it is the will of Allah (God) that he should own these riches, as Allah is the one who bestows wealth on all.

Gold bracelets

Gold bangles studded with jewels

Egyptian dinar: 1369

Iraqi dinar: 1203

A gold dinar was a valuable Arabic coin. One dinar equalled twenty dirhams – and only one dirham could buy five loaves of bread.

51

It didn't take long for Kasim's wife to find the coin.

Heaps of gold
A measuring scoop was a large spoon used to measure spices, grain, sugar, and flour. The fact that Ali Baba's wife uses a scoop to measure gold coins, rather than counting them, shows how much money she and Ali Baba now possess.

"Please my dear," said Ali Baba's wife sweetly, "may I borrow your measuring scoop? I promise I'll bring it back."

"What's it for?"

Ali Baba's wife sealed her lips. "It's a secret."

"Oh, is it now?" said Kasim's wife, rubbing her nose suspiciously. Turning her back, she smeared some sticky suet over the bottom of her measure, then handed it over.

Ali Baba's wife ran happily back to her own house, where Ali Baba had just finished digging the hole.

"Wait!" cried his wife. She began to scoop heaps of gold coins into the borrowed measure. Carefully, she counted each scoopful, then she tossed the coins into the hole.

As soon as this was done, and the hole filled in, she rushed back to return the measure to Kasim's wife. She didn't realize that a gold coin was stuck in the suet on the bottom.

It didn't take long for Kasim's wife to find the coin. "Kasim!" she shouted. "Come here!"

In he came.

"That pathetic brother of yours has got hold of a hoard of gold!" she shrieked at him. "There's so much of it that they scoop it up and measure it like flour! But do you think they've offered to share it with us? No, not one little bit! Go round there at once, husband, and make Ali Baba give you some gold, as a brother should!"

So Kasim rolled out and round the corner to Ali Baba's house. "What's this I hear?" complained Kasim. "My own brother coming into a fortune, and not giving his only relations a share-out? You should be ashamed of yourself, Ali Baba!"

"Ah ... um ... of course ... " stammered Ali Baba, making furious faces at his wife. "I was just about to come round and tell you all about it, Kasim. In fact, you can go and get some for yourself, brother, more than you could dream of. Just listen ... "

And he told Kasim all about the robbers' cave.

Now, Kasim was a greedy man – much greedier than Ali Baba. "I'm off to that cave," he cried, flinging open the door. "I'm going to help myself to everything I want!" He dashed home, collected ten mules, and hurried them through the forest to the magic rock.

"OPEN, SESAME!" he commanded. The rock opened up, he went in, and it slid discreetly shut behind him.

Inside, surrounded by all the treasure, the delicious sweets, and the flagons of rich old wine, Kasim began to dribble with excitement. He seized fistfuls of this and armfuls of that; dumping them by the rock face. Soon he was too tired to fetch more. He swaggered back.

"OPEN ... !" Oh dear, he couldn't remember the other word!

"I know it's something you can eat," he said. "Let me see now: OPEN, BARLEY!"

Nothing happened.

"Um ... OPEN, OATS!"

Still nothing.

"Er ... OPEN, RICE! OPEN, CORN! OPEN, BEANS!"

But the rock stayed shut.

"What am I going to do?" Kasim broke into a cold sweat. "Help, help, let me out!" He punched the rock, he kicked it, he stormed around the cave. He slapped the walls, he felt desperately for a crack. But it was no good. He began to cry.

Meanwhile, outside:

Da-dum. Da-dum, da-dum, da-dum.

The robbers were back.

The first thing they saw was Kasim's line of mules.

"Someone's sneaked on us!" they yelled, leaping from their horses and unsheathing their swords.

"OPEN, SESAME!" bellowed their chief. The rock slid open, and they burst in.

Kasim heard them coming. He tried to hide; but the wily robbers soon found him. He didn't even have time to beg for mercy. Out came their forty swords – and chopped him into little pieces.

Kasim desperately tried to remember the password.

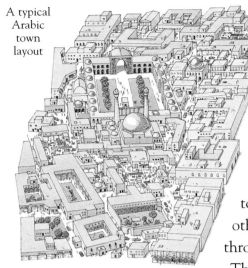

A typical Arabic town layout

Maze of streets
Many Arabic towns followed a similar pattern – a maze of narrow streets radiating out from a mosque in the centre. The robbers found it easy to hide round street-corners and listen to gossip.

Arabic hospitality
Ali Baba welcomes the disguised robber-chief into his home, reflecting the custom in Arabic countries of offering hospitality to strangers.

The robbers squatted amongst the litter of gold-dust and diamond-chips, fuming. To think that someone had discovered their secret!

"I bet that weakling we've just killed was working for someone else," sneered the chief. "We'll have to dig the other worm out, wherever he's hiding, and chop him up, like the first one."

So the robbers became spies. They sneaked round the town, here and there, listening at street corners, prying into other people's gossip; until one thing and another led them through the sun-baked maze of streets to Ali Baba's house.

The robber-chief trimmed his gruesome beard, and dressed himself up, until he was disguised as a respectable merchant. He went to a local pottery stall and bought forty enormous jars, slung two-by-two from a team of broad-backed horses.

Then he made the thirty-nine other thieves undress down to their swords and turbans, and climb into the jars, where they crouched quietly like trussed-up chickens. He filled up the fortieth jar with olive oil. He also smeared some oil round the rims of the other jars, so that it looked as if they were all full of the same thing.

Then he led the horses to Ali Baba's house and knocked politely on the door.

"Good evening, my dear friend," he said silkily when Ali Baba answered it. "I am a travelling dealer in high quality olive oil. I wonder if you know of anywhere that I could spend the night?"

"Of course, of course," cried Ali Baba, "you are very welcome to stay here with me." He didn't see beyond the robber-chief's disguise. He led the villain into his house, gave him a fine meal, and showed him to the guest room.

Meanwhile, his servants led the horses into the courtyard, gave them food and water, unloaded the heavy jars from their backs, and settled them down for the night.

Nobody realized that each jar contained a wicked robber polishing a deadly sword, just waiting for the signal from his chief to leap out and stab Ali Baba to death.

However, Ali Baba had a servant girl called Marjana, who had more brains and courage than the rest of the household put together. Long after the others had all gone to bed, this Marjana was still working hard clearing up after the feast. She was really tired – and then suddenly her lamp ran out of oil and went out.

"There's loads of oil out in the courtyard," she thought to herself. "I don't see why I shouldn't nip outside and help myself to some."

So she slipped quietly out to the nearest jar and dipped in a cup. But instead of olive oil, her cup bumped hard against one of the robbers' heads!

Olives must ripen to black before they can be used for oil.

Jars of oil
Olive oil made from pressed black olives was the common type of oil used in cooking and for lighting lamps. The oil was transported and stored in large earthenware jars.

Insead of olive oil, Marjana's cup bumped hard against one of the robbers' heads!

Marjana
Early versions of the story say that Marjana the slave girl was taken in as a baby by Ali Baba and his wife, and was brought up with as much love as if she had been their own child. It is out of loyalty to her owners that Marjana resorts to such desperate measures to defeat the robbers.

Dancer
From ten years old, female slaves were trained to perform as dancers, singers, and musicians to entertain guests at feasts and social gatherings. Marjana uses her dancing skills to defeat the robber-chief.

"Eeek!" Marjana almost jumped out of her skin. Then she noticed the gleam of a sword lifting up the lid of a jar ever so slightly, and other swords gleaming in other jars …

Marjana knew all about Ali Baba's secret hoard of treasure. She knew how Kasim had left in search of some, and never come back. It did not take her long to work out who these brutes were – and what they had come here to do.

A cunning smile spread across her face.

She tiptoed round the yard, peeping into all the jars. She pretended not to see the robbers, and the robbers pretended not to see her. At last she found the jar that really was full of oil.

She fetched a huge pot, filled it with oil, and put it over the fire until it was bubbling and boiling. Carefully, she poured the deadly hot liquid into the other jars, one by one, over the robbers' heads.

"AAGH!"

And that was the end of the robbers.

A little later, the chief woke up in the guest-room and threw a handful of pebbles into the courtyard. This was his sign to the gang to sneak up on the sleeping Ali Baba and stab him to death. But no one appeared and nothing happened, so he crept downstairs to wake them up.

When he reached the courtyard and found all his men cooked to frazzles in the boiling oil, he cast around for the culprit. Almost at once, his eye fell upon Marjana, who had finished her chores at last and was on her way to bed.

Marjana glanced around – just as the chief was about to pounce on her. Quickly she wriggled away and through some curtains to a little lamp-lit room. There she spied the things she needed. Within seconds she had changed out of her servant's clothes and was dressed as a dancing girl, covered in gold and sequins, whilst from her belt there dangled a gold-handled dancer's dagger.

The robber-chief stared in wonder as Marjana, chanting a slow, mesmerizing rhythm, emerged from the room and began to dance and sway before him. Then she pulled the dagger from its sheath and swung it to and fro before his face, intending to hypnotize him with the flickering, flashing blade.

But the wicked chief leaped forwards and tried to wrest the dagger from her. Marjana, struggling to save her life, managed to wrench her hand from his grasp and thrust the dagger straight into his abominable heart.

When Ali Baba came upon the scene, he was filled with horror. "What have you done?" he cried to Marjana. But once he heard that his honoured guest was in fact the chief of the forty robbers and that Marjana had saved his life, he was overcome with gratitude and he offered his son to her in marriage.

A year later, Ali Baba felt it was safe to return to the robbers' cave, with Marjana and his son. They found the site completely overgrown. Once more, Ali Baba cried out, "OPEN, SESAME!" and the rock face opened up. They ventured inside and helped themselves to the vast treasures that lay there.

After that, they never went near the place again, but they all had enough treasure to live like kings and queens for the rest of their days.

Persian dagger and holder made of steel with gold inlay.

Dagger
Arabic and Persian dancers sometimes performed their dance routines armed with swords or daggers, so that the blades swung out and mimicked the dancers' movements. Marjana cleverly uses this custom to her advantage.

Marjana began to dance and sway before the robber-chief.

57

In this story, a fisherman's courage and ingenuity are tested by an evil jinnee.

Arabic fishermen
Fishermen led a hard life. They worked from early morning till late afternoon – sometimes without catching a single fish. Arabic fishermen believed that any big catch was a reward from Allah for their patience.

King Solomon and the jinn
King of the jinn
According to Islamic legend, the biblical King Solomon had a signet ring inscribed with Allah's name which gave him power over the jinn. This jinnee is based on Sakhr al-Jinnee, whom Solomon had imprisoned in a jar for disobeying Allah.

THE FISHERMAN
and the
JINNEE

THERE WAS ONCE a poor fisherman who pulled his net out of the sea, and found nothing inside it – except an enormous jar. It was a fine antique, made of burnished, flame-red copper; and it was closed fast at the top with a heavy lid.

The fisherman was delighted and shouted his thanks to Allah, thinking he could get quite a bit of money if he sold it in the market. But first, he thought he should open it up and find out if there was anything of value inside.

The lid was tightly sealed: he had to work hard with his knife to get it loose. Then suddenly it came free – and before he knew what was happening, a great cloud of foul-smelling smoke burst from the jar and billowed up into the air.

The fisherman's eyes stung: he coughed and almost choked. Desperately he tried to stop the spell and push the lid back in place – but it was too late. As he cowered beneath it, the smoke began to swirl and solidify into strange, ill-omened patterns. Finally, settling into ominous stillness, it took on the unmistakable shape of a jinnee.

The fisherman guessed at once that this jinnee was a dangerous, evil creature. It was almost as tall as the sky, with burning coals instead of eyes and pronged claws for hands; its cavernous mouth gaped open in a leering, twisted grin.

"Listen!" it roared at him, "I bring you important news!"

The poor fisherman, squatting and trembling in the jinnee's shadow could only gabble, "Oh … oh …! P …p … please tell me Sir, what news is this?"

Slowly, the jinnee bent down, until its grotesque face loomed right over the fisherman's. It belched up the pungent smell of camel-dung.

"This is my news, you creeping, boneless maggot of a man,"
it hissed at him. "Today you are going to die!"

"But ... but ... why me?" stammered the fisherman. "What ...
what have I done to offend you?"

"You have freed me too late!" roared the jinnee. "Had you let
me out a thousand years ago, I might have granted you the
three dearest wishes of your heart's desire. Had you even
rescued me a hundred years ago, I may have showered
you with precious pearls, silver, and gold. But
no: you kept me waiting inside that
cramped, degrading prison for so
long that I must take my
revenge by torturing you
to death!"

*The smoke
settled and took on
the unmistakable
shape of a jinnee.*

The fisherman cast his net …

The fisherman quickly saw that he stood no chance of winning a fight or even an argument against this demon. So he searched through his mind for the well-spring of cunning: and then he said hoarsely:

"Sir, I … I … don't believe you. You could never have been stuck inside that little jar. You're far too mighty, much too big – it's impossible!"

"What?" bellowed the jinnee. "Do you dare to call me a liar?"

"I do Sir," whispered the fisherman.

"*Of course* I was in the jar!" roared the jinnee. "You saw me!"

"No I didn't," insisted the fisherman. "The smoke was too thick. I couldn't see anything through it."

"No one from heaven above to hell beneath shall ever accuse me of lying!" The jinnee had turned purple; it gnashed its teeth and began to spin round and round, in a dizzying, dazzling dance. "I shall prove to you, maggot-man, just how easily I can fit myself back into that jar. And as soon as you have applauded my trick, I shall leap out again, bite your head off, and tear you into tiny pieces!"

Round and round he whirled; down and down he shrank. He shivered and shook, coiled and contorted, back, back into the hollow darkness of the copper jar.

"You have seen me do it, eh?" it called. "So – back I come – I'm coming out … COMING TO GET YOU – NOW!"

But at that very moment, the fisherman leaped forward, snatched up the lid and rammed it in place so tightly that no power on Earth could have forced it out. Then he flung the jar out into the sea.

Ah, but what mysteries lurk in the deep!

As the seething water settled, the trembling fisherman thought that he was staring into a whirlpool of dancing rainbows. Slowly, the dark ripples gave way to light – and then he saw that the rainbows were really fish: ice-white and scarlet, lapis-blue, yellow, purple, and emerald-green.

The fisherman flung away the last of his fear and quickly got to work. He cast his net amongst them; and when he hauled it out, it was weighed down by one enormous fish of each colour. Into his basket he tossed them, all slithery and shimmery; then away he went, with great daring, to offer them for sale at no less a place than the royal palace.

His courage and quick thinking were not in vain. For the king's chief cook accepted them; and when they had been prepared and served on a marble platter, the king declared that these beautiful creatures tasted sweeter and more delicate than any other food on Earth. He was so delighted that he rewarded the fisherman with a huge purse crammed full to the brim with golden coins.

As for that evil jinnee, by now his copper jar had tumbled down and down, to stick fast in the mud that lies in the murkiest depths of the sea bed; and to this day neither ill-luck nor magic has ever set him free.

… and hauled out one enormous fish of each colour.

61

THE STORY OF THE STORIES

Professional storytellers were frequent visitors to the busy market-places of the Middle East. The tales they told of romance, adventure, and fantasy gave ordinary people a chance to escape into another world. From the 9th century, some of these stories began to be collected and written down – and later came to be known as the *Arabian Nights*, or the *Thousand and One Nights*. Translated into many languages, the tales have appeared on film, in cartoons, and on stage, and are known and loved throughout the world.

STORIES TO ENTERTAIN

Storytellers, or rawis, visited market squares and coffee houses where they competed with snake-charmers, jugglers, and pedlars for attention and for money from the crowds. Over time, these stories were written down and collected. There is no single original edition of the Nights in Arabic, but by the 18th century, numerous collections had been made. Each collection included a varied mix of fables, poetry, and heroic epics, as well as tales of fantasy, and they all shared one common feature: the tales were said to have been told by Shahrazad to her husband the king over 1,001 nights.

Men relaxing and smoking as they listen to the storyteller.

Translators of the Nights

The Arabic collections varied in content – one major version appeared in Cairo in the 18th century, but this did not include such stories as *Aladdin* or *Ali Baba*. The *Nights* were first introduced to Europe by the Frenchman Antoine Galland, a storyteller and Middle Eastern scholar. His book was published in 12 volumes in 1704–17, and proved very popular. Some of the stories, including *Ali Baba* and *Aladdin*, were told to him in France by an Arab named Hanna.

Richard Burton

The best-known translation into English is by the soldier, academic, and explorer Richard Burton, born in Torquay, England. Burton was one of the best-informed students of Islamic and Middle Eastern life of his time. In 1853 he disguised himself as an Arab pilgrim and became one of the first Europeans to enter the holy Islamic city of Mecca. His translation in 16 volumes was first published in 1885–88.

Richard Burton (1821–90)

Children's editions

Though originally intended for adults, most people have come to know the *Arabian Nights* through the many shorter editions retold for children, for whom the exotic settings, strong plots, and magical themes have a strong appeal. These collections frequently included *Sindbad the Sailor*, *Aladdin*, *Ali Baba*, and the frame story of Shahrazad.

A 1933 illustration by Arthur Rackha[m] of Sindbad an[d] the Old Mar[n] of the Sea, in which Sindba[d] becomes an ol[d] man's slave.

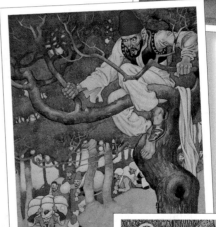

Ali Baba hiding in a tree, in this painting by Monro Orr.

This illustration by Walter Crane shows the princess about to give the magic lamp to the magician in Aladdin.

There have been many film versions of the Arabian Nights – notable for their colourful characterization and sense of fun rather than their faithfulness to the original plots. The tales adapted most often – Aladdin, Ali Baba, and Sindbad the Sailor – are known throughout the world and their principal characters have become household names.

The Thief of Baghdad

Probably the best version of the *Arabian Nights* on film is *The Thief of Baghdad* (1940). Although it differs wildly from the tales themselves, it comes the closest in capturing the wonderful, rich atmosphere of the stories, with its spectacular mix of action, humour, special effects, extravagant characters, colourful costumes, and rousing music.

... and is nearly crushed by a giant foot, in The Thief of Baghdad *(1940).*

Abu the thief hitches a ride from the giant jinnee ...

Cartoon

© Disney

Walt Disney's animated version of *Aladdin* (1992) featured innovative computer animation and the voice of American comic-actor Robin Williams as the jinnee.

Other films

Ali Baba and the Forty Thieves (1944, above) – in which a prince pretends to be a bandit in order to defeat his enemies – had very little to do with the original story, but does at least feature bandits hiding in earthenware jars!

The flying carpet is a magical device which appears in several of the tales, shown here in the film Arabian Adventure *(1979).*

Acknowledgements

Picture Credits
The publisher would like to thank the following for their kind permission to reproduce their photographs.

t=top, b=bottom, a=above,
c=centre, l=left, r=right.

AKG London: 58tl.
Pauline Baynes: 7, 19tr.
Chester Beatty Library: (Ms. 212, f.418v) 58bl, (Ms. 212, f.158b) 25tr, (Ms. 279, f.18v) 54bl, (Ms. 212, f.425) 25cr, (Ms.212, f.416v) 25br.
Chris Beetles Ltd: George Soper 56tl.
Bridgeman Art Library: Anthony Crane Collection 62br; British Library, London 8br; Chris Beetles Ltd, London 9tl; Louvre, Paris, France 22tl; Mander & Mitchenson Theatre Collection 63br; Musée Condé, Chantilly (Ms.206/1039) 8bl; Orleans House Gallery, Twickenham 62bl; Private Collection 9tr; Stapleton Collection 11tr, 30bl; Topkapi Palace Museum, Istanbul / Giraudon 41tr; Victoria & Albert Museum, London 13tr, 15tr, 39tr, 44tl.
British Library: (Add. 6810, f.190) 28cl; (Add. 6613, f.29b) 12bl; (Or.11676, f.520a) 9bc; (Or.1362, f.315a) 48tl.
British Museum: 8bc, 11cr (below), 21br, 21cr, 22bl, 33tr, 34cl, 35tr, 41cr, 51tr, 51cr, 51br, 53cr, 57tr.
Natural History Museum: 28tl, 40bl.
Christie's Images: 8c, 11cr, 16bl, 56bl, 62cl.

Bruce Coleman Ltd: Jane Burton 45br.
Mary Evans Picture Library: 10bl, 10cl (below), 17tr, 36bl, 62cr, 62cr (above).
Ronald Grant Archive: 63cl.
Sonia Halliday Photographs: 26cl, 26tl.
Robert Harding Picture Library: 42bl.
Bodleian Library (Mss. Ms. Ashmole) 44bl; J Perno & CD Tetrel 12tl.
Kobal Collection: 1940, Korda 63cl (above), 63tr; 1979, Badger Films / John Dark 63bc; Walt Disney Pictures 63cr.
Peter Sanders: 8tl.
Sotheby's Transparency Library: 10cl, 15br.
Tony Stone Images: Anthony Cassidy 42tl; Keren Su 20tl; Nabeel Turner 2tc; Nick Dolding 52cl.

Jacket:
Bridgeman Art Library: Louvre, Paris, France Back Jacket tc, Stapleton Collection Back Jacket cl (above).
British Library: (Add. 6810, f.190) Back Jacket br.
British Museum: Front Jacket tl, tr; Back Jacket cr (below), tc (right), cl (inset).
Circa Photo Library: back jacket cl.
Mary Evans Picture Library: back jacket cr (above).

Additional photography: John Williams, Kevin Lovelock, and Dudley Hubbard at the British Museum.

Additional illustrations: Philip Argent (58–9, 60–1), Philip Hood, Sallie Alane Reason, John Woodcock.
Calligraphy: Stephen Raw.

Dorling Kindersley would particularly like to thank the following people:

Lizzie Bacon for research assistance; Lynn Bresler for proofreading; the Oriental Antiquities department and the Coins and Medals department at the British Museum; Sheilagh Noble for visualization; Jane Thomas for design assistance.